THE TALE OF
MR TOD

THE TALE OF
Mᴿ TOD

BY

BEATRIX POTTER

Author of
" The Tale of Peter Rabbit," etc.

FREDERICK WARNE

*The reproductions in this book have been made using
the most modern electronic scanning methods from entirely
new transparencies of Beatrix Potter's original watercolours.
They enable Beatrix Potter's skill as an artist to be appreciated
as never before, not even during her own lifetime.*

FREDERICK WARNE

Penguin Books Ltd, Harmondsworth, Middlesex, England
Viking Penguin Inc., 40 West 23rd Street, New York, New York 10010, U.S.A.
Penguin Books Australia Ltd, Ringwood, Victoria, Australia
Penguin Books Canada Limited, 2801 John Street, Markham, Ontario, Canada L3R 1B4
Penguin Books (N.Z.) Ltd, 182–190 Wairau Road, Auckland 10, New Zealand

First published 1912
This edition with new reproductions first published 1987

Colour reproduction by
East Anglian Engraving Company Ltd, Norwich
Printed and bound in Great Britain by
William Clowes Limited, Beccles and London

0287

THE TALE OF MR TOD

I HAVE made many books about well-behaved people. Now, for a change, I am going to make a story about two disagreeable people, called Tommy Brock and Mr. Tod.

Nobody could call Mr. Tod "nice." The rabbits could not bear him ; they could smell him half a mile off. He was of a wandering habit and he had foxey whiskers ; they never knew where he would be next.

One day he was living in a stick-house in the coppice, causing terror to the family of old Mr. Benjamin Bouncer. Next day he moved into a pollard willow near the lake, frightening the wild ducks and the water rats.

In winter and early spring he might generally be found in an earth amongst the rocks at the top of Bull Banks, under Oatmeal Crag.

He had half a dozen houses, but he was seldom at home.

The houses were not always empty when Mr. Tod moved *out;* because sometimes Tommy Brock moved *in;* (without asking leave).

Tommy Brock was a short bristly fat waddling person with a grin; he grinned all over his face. He was not nice in his habits. He ate wasp nests and frogs and worms; and he waddled about by moonlight, digging things up.

His clothes were very dirty; and as he slept in the day-time, he always went to bed in his boots. And the bed which he went to bed in, was generally Mr. Tod's.

Now Tommy Brock did occasionally eat rabbit-pie; but it was only very little young ones occasionally, when other food was really scarce. He was friendly with old Mr. Bouncer; they agreed in disliking the wicked otters and Mr. Tod; they often talked over that painful subject.

Old Mr. Bouncer was stricken in years. He sat in the spring sunshine outside the burrow, in a muffler; smoking a pipe of rabbit tobacco.

He lived with his son Benjamin Bunny and his daughter-in-law Flopsy, who had a young family. Old Mr. Bouncer was in charge of the family that afternoon, because Benjamin and Flopsy had gone out.

The little rabbit-babies were just old enough to open their blue eyes and kick. They lay in a fluffy bed of rabbit wool and hay, in a shallow burrow, separate from the main rabbit hole. To tell the truth—old Mr. Bouncer had forgotten them.

He sat in the sun, and conversed cordially with Tommy Brock, who was passing through the wood with a sack and a little spud which he used for digging, and some mole traps. He complained bitterly about the

scarcity of pheasants' eggs, and accused Mr. Tod of poaching them. And the otters had cleared off all the frogs while he was asleep in winter—" I have not had a good square meal for a fortnight, I am living on pig-nuts. I shall have to turn vegetarian and eat my own tail ! " said Tommy Brock.

It was not much of a joke, but it tickled old Mr. Bouncer ; because Tommy Brock was so fat and stumpy and grinning.

So old Mr. Bouncer laughed; and pressed Tommy Brock to come inside, to taste a slice of seed-cake and " a glass of my daughter Flopsy's cowslip wine." Tommy Brock squeezed himself into the rabbit hole with alacrity.

Then old Mr. Bouncer smoked another pipe, and gave Tommy Brock a cabbage leaf cigar which was so very strong that it made Tommy Brock grin more than ever; and the smoke filled the burrow. Old Mr. Bouncer coughed and laughed; and Tommy Brock puffed and grinned.

And Mr. Bouncer laughed and coughed, and shut his eyes because of the cabbage smoke . . . .

When Flopsy and Benjamin came back—old Mr. Bouncer woke up. Tommy Brock and all the young rabbit-babies had disappeared!

Mr. Bouncer would not confess that he had admitted anybody into the rabbit hole. But the smell of badger was undeniable ; and there were round heavy footmarks in the sand. He was in disgrace ; Flopsy wrung her ears, and slapped him.

Benjamin Bunny set off at once after Tommy Brock.

There was not much difficulty in tracking him ; he had left his footmark and gone slowly up the winding footpath through the wood. Here he had rooted up the moss and wood sorrel. There he had dug quite a deep hole for dog darnel ; and had set a mole trap. A little stream crossed the way. Benjamin skipped lightly over dry-foot ; the badger's heavy steps showed plainly in the mud.

The path led to a part of the thicket where the trees had been cleared ; there were leafy oak stumps, and a sea of blue hyacinths—but the smell that made Benjamin stop, was *not* the smell of flowers !

Mr. Tod's stick house was before him and, for once, Mr. Tod was at home. There was not only a foxey flavour in proof of it—there was smoke coming out of the broken pail that served as a chimney.

Benjamin Bunny sat up, staring ; his whiskers twitched. Inside the stick house somebody dropped a plate, and said something. Benjamin stamped his foot, and bolted.

He never stopped till he came to
the other side of the wood. Appa-
rently Tommy Brock had turned
the same way. Upon the top of the
wall, there were again the marks of
badger ; and some ravellings of a
sack had caught on a briar.

Benjamin climbed over the wall,
into a meadow. He found another
mole trap newly set ; he was still
upon the track of Tommy Brock.
It was getting late in the afternoon.
Other rabbits were coming out to
enjoy the evening air. One of them
in a blue coat by himself, was busily
hunting for dandelions.—" Cousin
Peter! Peter Rabbit, Peter Rabbit!"
shouted Benjamin Bunny.

The blue coated rabbit sat up
with pricked ears—

" Whatever is the matter, Cousin Benjamin ? Is it a cat ? or John Stoat Ferret ? "

" No, no, no ! He's bagged my family—Tommy Brock—in a sack —have you seen him ? "

" Tommy Brock ? how many, Cousin Benjamin ? "

" Seven, Cousin Peter, and all of them twins ! Did he come this way ? Please tell me quick ! "

" Yes, yes ; not ten minutes since
. . . . he said they were *caterpillars;*
I did think they were kicking rather
hard, for caterpillars."

" Which way ? which way has he
gone, Cousin Peter ? "

" He had a sack with something
'live in it ; I watched him set a
mole trap. Let me use my mind,
Cousin Benjamin ; tell me from the
beginning." Benjamin did so.

"My Uncle Bouncer has displayed a lamentable want of discretion for his years;" said Peter reflectively, " but there are two hopeful circumstances. Your family is alive and kicking; and Tommy Brock has had refreshment. He will probably go to sleep, and keep them for breakfast." " Which way?" " Cousin Benjamin, compose yourself. I know very well which way. Because Mr. Tod was at home in the stick-house he has gone to Mr. Tod's other house, at the top of Bull Banks. I partly know, because he offered to leave any message at Sister Cottontail's; he said he would be passing." (Cottontail had married a black rabbit, and gone to live on the hill).

Peter hid his dandelions, and accompanied the afflicted parent, who was all of a twitter. They crossed several fields and began to climb the hill ; the tracks of Tommy Brock were plainly to be seen. He seemed to have put down the sack every dozen yards, to rest.

" He must be very puffed ; we are close behind him, by the scent. What a nasty person ! " said Peter.

The sunshine was still warm and slanting on the hill pastures. Half way up, Cottontail was sitting in her doorway, with four or five half-grown little rabbits playing about her; one black and the others brown.

Cottontail had seen Tommy Brock passing in the distance. Asked whether her husband was at home she replied that Tommy Brock had rested twice while she watched him.

He had nodded, and pointed to the sack, and seemed doubled up with laughing. — " Come away, Peter ; he will be cooking them ; come quicker ! " said Benjamin Bunny.

They climbed up and up ;—" He was at home ; I saw his black ears peeping out of the hole." " They live too near the rocks to quarrel with their neighbours. Come on, Cousin Benjamin ! "

When they came near the wood at the top of Bull Banks, they went cautiously. The trees grew amongst heaped up rocks; and there, beneath a crag—Mr. Tod had made one of his homes. It was at the top of a steep bank ; the rocks and bushes overhung it. The rabbits crept up carefully, listening and peeping.

This house was something between a cave, a prison, and a tumble-down pig-stye. There was a strong door, which was shut and locked.

The setting sun made the window panes glow like red flame ; but the kitchen fire was not alight. It was neatly laid with dry sticks, as the rabbits could see, when they peeped through the window.

Benjamin sighed with relief.

But there were preparations upon the kitchen table which made him shudder. There was an immense empty pie-dish of blue willow pattern, and a large carving knife and fork, and a chopper.

At the other end of the table was a partly unfolded tablecloth, a plate, a tumbler, a knife and fork, salt-cellar, mustard and a chair—in short, preparations for one person's supper.

No person was to be seen, and
no young rabbits. The kitchen was
empty and silent ; the clock had run
down. Peter and Benjamin flattened
their noses against the window, and
stared into the dusk.

Then they scrambled round the
rocks to the other side of the house.
It was damp and smelly, and over-
grown with thorns and briars.

The rabbits shivered in their shoes.

"Oh my poor rabbit babies! What a dreadful place ; I shall never see them again ! " sighed Benjamin.

They crept up to the bedroom window. It was closed and bolted like the kitchen. But there were signs that this window had been recently open ; the cobwebs were disturbed, and there were fresh dirty footmarks upon the window-sill.

The room inside was so dark, that at first they could make out nothing; but they could hear a noise —a slow deep regular snoring grunt. And as their eyes became accustomed to the darkness, they perceived that somebody was asleep on Mr. Tod's bed, curled up under the blanket.—"He has gone to bed in his boots," whispered Peter.

Benjamin, who was all of a twitter, pulled Peter off the window-sill.

Tommy Brock's snores continued, grunty and regular from Mr. Tod's bed. Nothing could be seen of the young family.

The sun had set ; an owl began to hoot in the wood. There were many unpleasant things lying about, that had much better have been buried; rabbit bones and skulls, and chickens' legs and other horrors. It was a shocking place, and very dark.

They went back to the front of the house, and tried in every way to move the bolt of the kitchen window. They tried to push up a rusty nail between the window sashes ; but it was of no use, especially without a light.

They sat side by side outside the
window, whispering and listening.

In half an hour the moon rose
over the wood. It shone full and
clear and cold, upon the house
amongst the rocks, and in at the
kitchen window. But alas, no little
rabbit babies were to be seen !

The moonbeams twinkled on the
carving knife and the pie dish, and
made a path of brightness across
the dirty floor.

The light showed a little door in

a wall beside the kitchen fireplace—
a little iron door belonging to a
brick oven, of that old-fashioned
sort that used to be heated with
faggots of wood.

And presently at the same moment
Peter and Benjamin noticed that
whenever they shook the window—
the little door opposite shook in
answer. The young family were
alive ; shut up in the oven !

Benjamin was so excited that it was a mercy he did not awake Tommy Brock, whose snores continued solemnly in Mr. Tod's bed.

But there really was not very much comfort in the discovery. They could not open the window; and although the young family was alive—the little rabbits were quite incapable of letting themselves out ; they were not old enough to crawl.

After much whispering, Peter and Benjamin decided to dig a tunnel. They began to burrow a yard or two lower down the bank. They hoped that they might be able to work between the large stones under the house; the kitchen floor was so dirty that it was impossible to say whether it was made of earth or flags.

They dug and dug for hours. They could not tunnel straight on account of stones ; but by the end of the night they were under the kitchen floor. Benjamin was on his back, scratching upwards. Peter's claws were worn down ; he was outside the tunnel, shuffling sand away. He called out that it was morning—sunrise ; and that the jays were making a noise down below in the woods.

Benjamin Bunny came out of the dark tunnel, shaking the sand from his ears ; he cleaned his face with his paws. Every minute the sun shone warmer on the top of the hill. In the valley there was a sea of white mist, with golden tops of trees showing through.

Again from the fields down below in the mist there came the angry cry of a jay—followed by the sharp yelping bark of a fox !

Then those two rabbits lost their heads completely. They did the most foolish thing that they could have done. They rushed into their short new tunnel, and hid themselves at the top end of it, under Mr. Tod's kitchen floor.

Mr. Tod was coming up Bull
Banks, and he was in the very worst
of tempers. First he had been upset by breaking the plate. It was
his own fault ; but it was a china
plate, the last of the dinner service
that had belonged to his grand-
mother, old Vixen Tod. Then the
midges had been very bad. And he
had failed to catch a hen pheasant on
her nest; and it had contained only
five eggs, two of them addled. Mr.
Tod had had an unsatisfactory night.

As usual, when out of humour, he determined to move house. First he tried the pollard willow, but it was damp ; and the otters had left a dead fish near it. Mr. Tod likes nobody's leavings but his own.

He made his way up the hill; his temper was not improved by noticing unmistakable marks of badger. No one else grubs up the moss so wantonly as Tommy Brock.

Mr. Tod slapped his stick upon the earth and fumed ; he guessed where Tommy Brock had gone to. He was further annoyed by the jay bird which followed him persistently. It flew from tree to tree and scolded, warning every rabbit within hearing that either a cat or a fox was coming up the plantation. Once when it flew screaming over his head — Mr. Tod snapped at it, and barked.

He approached his house very carefully, with a large rusty key. He sniffed and his whiskers bristled. The house was locked up, but Mr. Tod had his doubts whether it was empty. He turned the rusty key in the lock ; the rabbits below could hear it. Mr. Tod opened the door cautiously and went in.

The sight that met Mr. Tod's eyes
in Mr. Tod's kitchen made Mr. Tod
furious. There was Mr. Tod's chair,
and Mr. Tod's pie dish, and his knife
and fork and mustard and salt cellar
and his table-cloth that he had left
folded up in the dresser—all set out
for supper (or breakfast)—without
doubt for that odious Tommy Brock.

There was a smell of fresh earth
and dirty badger, which fortunately

overpowered all smell of rabbit.

But what absorbed Mr. Tod's attention was a noise—a deep slow regular snoring grunting noise, coming from his own bed.

He peeped through the hinges of the half-open bedroom door. Then he turned and came out of the house in a hurry. His whiskers bristled and his coat-collar stood on end with rage.

For the next twenty minutes Mr. Tod kept creeping cautiously into the house, and retreating hurriedly out again. By degrees he ventured further in—right into the bedroom. When he was outside the house, he scratched up the earth with fury. But when he was inside—he did not like the look of Tommy Brock's teeth.

He was lying on his back with his mouth open, grinning from ear to ear. He snored peacefully and regularly ; but one eye was not perfectly shut.

Mr. Tod came in and out of the bedroom. Twice he brought in his walking-stick, and once he brought in the coal-scuttle. But he thought better of it, and took them away.

When he came back after removing the coal-scuttle, Tommy Brock was lying a little more sideways; but he seemed even sounder asleep. He was an incurably indolent person; he was not in the least afraid of Mr. Tod; he was simply too lazy and comfortable to move.

Mr. Tod came back yet again into the bedroom with a clothes line. He stood a minute watching Tommy Brock and listening attentively to the snores. They were very loud indeed, but seemed quite natural.

Mr. Tod turned his back towards the bed, and undid the window. It creaked; he turned round with a jump. Tommy Brock, who had opened one eye—shut it hastily. The snores continued.

Mr. Tod's proceedings were peculiar, and rather uneasy, (because the bed was between the window and the door of the bedroom). He opened the window a little way, and pushed out the greater part of the clothes line on to the window sill. The rest of the line, with a hook at the end, remained in his hand.

Tommy Brock snored conscientiously. Mr. Tod stood and looked at him for a minute ; then he left the room again.

Tommy Brock opened both eyes, and looked at the rope and grinned. There was a noise outside the window. Tommy Brock shut his eyes in a hurry.

Mr. Tod had gone out at the front door, and round to the back of the house. On the way, he stumbled over the rabbit burrow. If he had had any idea who was inside it, he would have pulled them out quickly.

His foot went through the tunnel nearly upon the top of Peter Rabbit and Benjamin, but fortunately he thought that it was some more of Tommy Brock's work.

He took up the coil of line from the sill, listened for a moment, and then tied the rope to a tree.

Tommy Brock watched him with one eye, through the window. He was puzzled.

Mr. Tod fetched a large heavy pailful of water from the spring, and staggered with it through the kitchen into his bedroom.

Tommy Brock snored industriously, with rather a snort.

Mr. Tod put down the pail beside the bed, took up the end of rope with the hook — hesitated, and looked at Tommy Brock. The snores were almost apoplectic ; but the grin was not quite so big.

Mr. Tod gingerly mounted a chair by the head of the bedstead. His legs were dangerously near to Tommy Brock's teeth.

He reached up and put the end of rope, with the hook, over the head of the tester bed, where the curtains ought to hang.

(Mr. Tod's curtains were folded up, and put away, owing to the house being unoccupied. So was the counterpane. Tommy Brock was covered with a blanket only.) Mr. Tod standing on the unsteady chair looked down upon him attentively ; he really was a first prize sound sleeper !

It seemed as though nothing would waken him—not even the flapping rope across the bed.

Mr. Tod descended safely from the chair, and endeavoured to get up again with the pail of water. He intended to hang it from the hook, dangling over the head of Tommy Brock, in order to make a sort of shower-bath, worked by a string, through the window.

But naturally being a thin-legged person (though vindictive and sandy whiskered)—he was quite unable to lift the heavy weight to the level of the hook and rope. He very nearly overbalanced himself.

The snores became more and more apoplectic. One of Tommy Brock's hind legs twitched under the blanket, but still he slept on peacefully.

Mr. Tod and the pail descended from the chair without accident. After considerable thought, he emptied the water into a wash-basin and jug. The empty pail was not too heavy for him ; he slung it up wobbling over the head of Tommy Brock.

Surely there never was such a sleeper ! Mr. Tod got up and down, down and up on the chair.

As he could not lift the whole pailful of water at once, he fetched a milk jug, and ladled quarts of water into the pail by degrees. The pail got fuller and fuller, and swung like a pendulum. Occasionally a drop splashed over; but still Tommy Brock snored regularly and never moved,—except one eye.

At last Mr. Tod's preparations were complete. The pail was full of water; the rope was tightly strained over the top of the bed, and across the window sill to the tree outside.

"It will make a great mess in my bedroom; but I could never sleep in that bed again without a spring cleaning of some sort," said Mr. Tod.

Mr. Tod took a last look at the badger and softly left the room. He went out of the house, shutting the front door. The rabbits heard his footsteps over the tunnel.

He ran round behind the house, intending to undo the rope in order to let fall the pailful of water upon Tommy Brock—

"I will wake him up with an unpleasant surprise," said Mr. Tod.

The moment he had gone, Tommy Brock got up in a hurry ; he rolled Mr. Tod's dressing-gown into a bundle, put it into the bed beneath the pail of water instead of himself, and left the room also—grinning immensely.

He went into the kitchen, lighted the fire and boiled the kettle ; for the moment he did not trouble himself to cook the baby rabbits.

When Mr. Tod got to the tree, he found that the weight and strain had dragged the knot so tight that it was past untying. He was obliged to gnaw it with his teeth. He chewed and gnawed for more than twenty minutes. At last the rope gave way with such a sudden jerk that it nearly pulled his teeth out, and quite knocked him over backwards.

Inside the house there was a great crash and splash, and the noise of a pail rolling over and over.

But no screams. Mr. Tod was mystified ; he sat quite still, and listened attentively. Then he peeped in at the window. The water was dripping from the bed, the pail had rolled into a corner.

In the middle of the bed under the blanket, was a wet flattened *something*—much dinged in, in the middle where the pail had caught it (as it were across the tummy). Its head was covered by the wet blanket and it was *not snoring any longer*.

There was nothing stirring, and no sound except the drip, drop, drop drip of water trickling from the mattress.

Mr. Tod watched it for half an hour; his eyes glistened.

Then he cut a caper, and became so bold that he even tapped at the window; but the bundle never moved.

Yes—there was no doubt about it—it had turned out even better than he had planned; the pail had hit poor old Tommy Brock, and killed him dead!

" I will bury that nasty person in the hole which he has dug. I will bring my bedding out, and dry it in the sun," said Mr. Tod.

" I will wash the tablecloth and spread it on the grass in the sun to bleach. And the blanket must be hung up in the wind ; and the bed must be thoroughly disinfected, and aired with a warming-pan ; and warmed with a hot-water bottle."

" I will get soft soap, and monkey soap, and all sorts of soap ; and soda and scrubbing brushes ; and persian powder ; and carbolic to remove the smell. I must have a disinfecting. Perhaps I may have to burn sulphur."

He hurried round the house to get a shovel from the kitchen— " First I will arrange the hole— then I will drag out that person in the blanket . . ."

He opened the door. . . .

Tommy Brock was sitting at Mr. Tod's kitchen table, pouring out tea from Mr. Tod's tea-pot into Mr. Tod's tea-cup. He was quite dry himself and grinning ; and he threw the cup of scalding tea all over Mr. Tod.

Then Mr. Tod rushed upon Tommy Brock, and Tommy Brock grappled with Mr. Tod amongst the broken crockery, and there was a terrific battle all over the kitchen. To the rabbits underneath it sounded as if the floor would give way at each crash of falling furniture.

They crept out of their tunnel, and hung about amongst the rocks and bushes, listening anxiously.

Inside the house the racket was fearful. The rabbit babies in the oven woke up trembling; perhaps it was fortunate they were shut up inside.

Everything was upset except the kitchen table.

And everything was broken, except the mantelpiece and the kitchen fender. The crockery was smashed to atoms.

The chairs were broken, and the window, and the clock fell with a crash, and there were handfuls of Mr. Tod's sandy whiskers.

The vases fell off the mantel-piece, the canisters fell off the shelf; the kettle fell off the hob. Tommy Brock put his foot in a jar of raspberry jam.

And the boiling water out of the kettle fell upon the tail of Mr. Tod.

When the kettle fell, Tommy Brock, who was still grinning, happened to be uppermost; and he rolled Mr. Tod over and over like a log, out at the door.

Then the snarling and worrying went on outside; and they rolled over the bank, and down hill, bumping over the rocks. There will never be any love lost between Tommy Brock and Mr. Tod.

As soon as the coast was clear, Peter Rabbit and Benjamin Bunny came out of the bushes—

" Now for it ! Run in, Cousin Benjamin ! Run in and get them ! while I watch at the door."

But Benjamin was frightened—

"Oh; oh! they are coming back!"

" No they are not."

" Yes they are ! "

" What dreadful bad language ! I think they have fallen down the stone quarry."

Still Benjamin hesitated, and Peter kept pushing him—

" Be quick, it's all right. Shut the oven door, Cousin Benjamin, so that he won't miss them."

Decidedly there were lively doings in Mr. Tod's kitchen !

At home in the rabbit hole, things had not been quite comfortable.

After quarrelling at supper, Flopsy and old Mr. Bouncer had passed a sleepless night, and quarrelled again at breakfast. Old Mr. Bouncer could no longer deny that he had invited company into the rabbit hole ; but he refused to reply to the questions and reproaches of Flopsy. The day passed heavily.

Old Mr. Bouncer, very sulky, was huddled up in a corner, barricaded with a chair. Flopsy had taken away his pipe and hidden the tobacco. She had been having a complete turn out and spring-cleaning, to relieve her feelings. She had just finished. Old Mr. Bouncer, behind his chair, was wondering anxiously what she would do next.

In Mr. Tod's kitchen, amongst the wreckage, Benjamin Bunny picked his way to the oven nervously, through a thick cloud of dust. He opened the oven door, felt inside, and found something warm and wriggling. He lifted it out carefully, and rejoined Peter Rabbit.

"I've got them! Can we get away? Shall we hide, Cousin Peter?"

Peter pricked his ears; distant sounds of fighting still echoed in the wood.

Five minutes afterwards two breathless rabbits came scuttering away down Bull Banks, half carrying half dragging a sack between them, bumpetty bump over the grass. They reached home safely and burst into the rabbit hole.

Great was old Mr. Bouncer's relief and Flopsy's joy when Peter and Benjamin arrived in triumph with the young family. The rabbit-babies were rather tumbled and very hungry ; they were fed and put to bed. They soon recovered.

A long new pipe and a fresh supply of rabbit tobacco was presented to Mr. Bouncer. He was rather upon his dignity ; but he accepted.

Old Mr. Bouncer was forgiven, and they all had dinner. Then Peter and Benjamin told their story—but they had not waited long enough to be able to tell the end of the battle between Tommy Brock and Mr. Tod.

THE END